LOON AND MOON
and Other Animal Stories

by Kevin Strauss
Illustrated by Nancy Scheibe

D1166005

Raven Productions, Inc
Ely, Minnesota

A note for professional storytellers:
I believe that stories are for telling, so you have my permission to tell these stories in live performances at schools, nature centers, camps, libraries, and community events as long as you credit me as the source. If you would like to record or reprint these stories in any form (including electronic, hard copy, or online), you must have written permission from both me and Raven Productions, Inc. Thank you. KS

Dedicated to my wonderful wife Andrea,
the northern light of my sky.

Library of Congress Cataloging-in-Publication Data

Strauss, Kevin, 1969-
  Loon and Moon and other animal stories / by Kevin Strauss ; illustrated by Nancy Scheibe.
    p. cm.
  ISBN 0-9766264-3-8 (alk. paper)
  1. Children's stories, American. 2. Animals--Juvenile fiction. [1. Animals--Fiction. 2. Short stories.] I. Scheibe, Nancy, 1956- ill. II. Title.

  PZ7.S91243Loon 2005
  [Fic]--dc22   2005029592

Text copyright © 2005 Kevin Strauss
Illustrations copyright © 2005 Nancy Scheibe
Published November, 2005 by Raven Productions, Inc. PO Box 188, Ely, MN 55731 • 218.365.3375   www.ravenwords.com

Printed in Minnesota, United States of America
10 9 8 7 6 5 4 3 2 1

Table of Contents

4   *Loon and Moon*

Loon and Moon

Long, long ago, some people say, Moon shone her full light onto the earth every night as she traveled across the dark night sky. The full moon helped the animals see where they were going. It helped them find their food and find their narrow paths through the woods.

Each night, Moon put on her moon shawl and set off across the sky. But it is a long way from one end of the sky to the other, and after shining so brightly every night, Moon began to tire. One night, she was so tired that she wasn't watching where she was going, and she tripped and fell off the sky road. She fell down and down and down and down and

SPLASH!

right into a lake.

Now you may not know this, but Moon can't swim. She sank like a stone (which is what she is), right to the bottom of that lake. The animals on the shore saw what happened and gathered at the lakeshore.

"What are we going to do!?   What are we going to do!?" called Flying Squirrel. "If we don't rescue Moon, our nights will be so dark that we won't be able to find our way around."

"Now don't worry," said Moose. "I'm sure someone could go out and rescue Moon."

The animals stared at the glowing lake waters. Finally Beaver spoke, "I'll try to rescue Moon. I'm a very good swimmer."

Saying that, Beaver waddled into the water and began kicking with his webbed hind feet and steering with his flat tail. He swam out to the middle of the lake, took a deep beaver breath, and dove down and down and down. He could see the moon getting bigger and brighter. But then Beaver's

lungs began to burn and his eyes felt squished into the back of his head. Moon was still a long way down, so Beaver turned and kicked for the surface.

POOSH!

he broke through the water.

"I couldn't do it," said Beaver, gasping for breath. "Someone else should try."

"Let me try," came a deep voice. It was Snapping Turtle. Slowly Turtle walked into the water and began swimming with his four webbed turtle feet. He swam out to the middle of the lake, took a deep turtle breath, and dove down and down and down. He could see the moon getting bigger and brighter and brighter and bigger as he swam closer. But then Turtle's lungs started to burn and his eyes felt squished into the back of his head. Even though he had gone deeper than Beaver, Turtle could go no further, so he turned and kicked for the surface. POOSH! he broke through the water.

"I couldn't do it," gasped Snapping Turtle. "Someone else should try."

The animals on shore all looked at each other. Some of them, like Moth, couldn't swim at all. Others, like Deer and Porcupine, could swim but couldn't hold their breath as long as Beaver or Turtle.

"Euu-oh, I could try. Euu-oh, I could try, I could try," said a soft voice.

The animals looked out at the lake where the voice had come from. In the dim starlight, they could barely make out the midnight black shape of Loon sitting in the water. Her jet black wings made her almost invisible in the night. You see, back then, Loon was all black like her cousin Raven.

" Euu-oh, I could try," Loon said again.

"Haw haw haw!" laughed Bear, his belly shaking with the effort. "Loon, you're only a bird. And birds never do anything important."

Some of the other animals laughed too, but Loon didn't pay any attention to them.

"Yes, it's true that I am a bird, but I am also a loon," she said.

And with that she opened her black wings and began to run and

flap and run and flap and run and flap and run and flap (Did you ever notice how long it takes for a loon to get airborne?) and run and flap and run and flap and run and flap and finally, she rose up and up and up into the air.

Now Loon knew from watching Beaver and Turtle that Moon was in the deepest part of the lake. She knew she couldn't dive that deep from the surface of the lake. She knew that to get that deep, she'd have to do something that loons never do—dive from the sky. She had watched her cousin Tern do that, so Loon decided to imitate Tern's dive.

Loon circled the lake three times climbing higher and higher with each loop. Then she turned toward the center. Loon pointed her bill at the soft glow from Moon, deep below the water. She closed her wings and dropped like an arrow into the water.

SPLASH! she hit the water and as soon as she did, she began kicking with those big webbed loon feet. She dove faster than a muskie, going deeper and deeper into that lake. She could see the white glow of Moon getting bigger and brighter and brighter and bigger as she got closer and closer to Moon. Soon, Loon began to feel her lungs burn and her eyes squish into the back of her head, but she didn't give up. She kept kicking and kicking until she reached out with her long bill and CLOMP! she grabbed on to Moon.

Loon pulled with all her strength and dragged Moon out of the mud. With Moon in her bill, Loon began kicking and flapping for the surface of the lake. Loon's muscles hurt like they had never hurt before. She felt lightheaded as if a shadow were covering her red eyes. But Loon summoned all of her remaining strength and she kicked one last time and POOSH! she broke through the surface of the lake.

Loon lay there on the water trying to catch her breath. She set Moon on her back, in the same way that she carries her chicks. As Loon was resting, Moon looked at her.

"Loon, you saved me. If it weren't for you, I would have been stuck in that mud forever. Let me give you a gift."

Saying that, Moon took off her shawl and tied it around Loon's neck with a white cord. The shawl had squares of white like the moon, and squares of black like the night.

"Now you and your children can wear my shawl as a sign of your bravery," said Moon.

Loon rested a little longer, then opened her wings once more and flew Moon back up to the sky road, so Moon could finish her journey.

From that day on, loons have had wings dressed with squares of white like the moon and black like the night, just like Moon's shawl. And since that time, Moon doesn't cross the sky every single night. You may have noticed that sometimes you see a full Moon, but other times you see a quarter or a half or no Moon at all. On those nights, people say that Moon is resting, because it is still a long way across the sky, and Moon learned a long time ago that she needs to pace herself and always watch where she's going. That's the way it was and that's the way it is and that's the end of the story.

Loon and Moon

This is an original story, but many northern cultures have stories about why the loon has its distinctive plumage.

The common name "loon" comes from an old Norwegian word for "lame." Loons' legs are set so far back on their bodies that they can't walk on land the way ducks and geese do. They push themselves along on their bellies. Except when they are nesting or migrating, loons live on the water.

Loons nest right at the shoreline where they can slide onto their nest from the water. This makes their eggs vulnerable to wakes from motor boats or to fluctuating water levels from dam activity.

Most birds have hollow bones, but loons have solid bones, making them heavier than other birds. With such a heavy body and short wings, a loon needs to get a good running start with lots of running and flapping to get airborne. Like an airplane, loons use wind to help them gain air speed and they need a "runway." On hot days a loon may get stuck on a small lake and have to wait for more wind or cooler temperatures before being able to take off.

Although their bodies may seem heavy and awkward on land, loons can dive deeper and swim faster than most other water birds. This helps them find and catch fish, which is their main source of food.

Loon and Moon

Goldenfur

Once upon a time, there was a young bear named Goldenfur. Unlike her black-furred mother and brother, Goldenfur's coat shone like the sun in the morning. One day, as Goldenfur was walking through the forest, she smelled an aroma she had never smelled before. She wasn't sure exactly what it was, but it made her mouth water. She licked her lips and set off in search of the smell.

Soon Goldenfur's nose led her to a clearing with a little cabin in its center. Goldenfur circled the building, watching and sniffing for danger. Then her appetite overcame her caution, and she headed straight toward the front porch and that wonderful smell. She walked through the screen door and into the cabin. The smell was even stronger now. Goldenfur sniffed her way to the kitchen and found what she was looking for - blueberry pies.

Goldenfur climbed onto the table and licked the first pie, but it was too hot. So she took a nibble of the second pie, and it was too cold. But she ate it anyway. Then she gobbled up the third pie, and it was just right. By that time, the first pie had cooled enough, so she slurped up that one, too.

"Mmmmm good," sighed a contented Goldenfur, licking the blueberries off of her snout.

Goldenfur had never seen a place like this before. There were shiny things and smelly things all over the room. After rooting through some strong-smelling cans of dark powders and leaves, Goldenfur noticed a strange yummy smell coming from the next room. She sniffed her way into the living room and climbed onto a wooden chair that reminded her of the branches she climbed in the woods. But the chair was too hard. And it didn't have anything yummy near it.

So Goldenfur climbed into a cushy recliner, but when she sat there, she didn't smell that yummy smell she was looking for. Then she saw a small rocking chair in the corner. The chair had a shiny bag on the seat, and inside the bag something smelled good. Goldenfur climbed onto that chair, tore the bag open with her claws, and picked up some potato chips with her long lips. They tasted salty and she liked that taste. But as she was struggling to get the last chip out of the bag, she leaned back on the chair and "Snap!" it broke, sending her tumbling onto the floor.

After eating three blueberry pies and a whole bag of potato chips, Goldenfur was feeling full and sleepy. So she walked into the next room and found two beds. She climbed onto the first bed and found it was a stiff futon. So she went to the other bed, but the blanket smelled sharp and made her nose burn. She had never smelled mothballs before.

Goldenfur left that room and went down the hall to another bedroom. The bed in that room felt soft and the blankets smelled like flower blossoms. She climbed onto the bed, curled up, and fell fast asleep.

While Goldenfur was sleeping, the family that lived in the cabin came home. They knew they had a visitor when they saw the torn screen door, the pie pans on the floor, and the broken chair in the living room. When they found Goldenfur snoring softly in the bedroom, they grabbed their camera.

Goldenfur awoke to a flash like lightning. She heard people noises and smelled people smells, and she felt scared. Her heart started to pound. She saw the people in the doorway. She was terrified!

Goldenfur looked around the room in a panic. There, through the window, was her forest. She jumped off the bed, right through the screen, and out the window. She ran for the woods, never looking back.

That was the last time that Goldenfur went anywhere near a place with people smells. But in that cabin there hangs a framed picture of a little blonde bear sound asleep on a child's bed.

Loon and Moon

This is a switched around version of the well-known English folktale "Goldilocks," about a little girl who makes herself at home in a cabin belonging to a bear family.

Black bears are often black, but they can also be brown, blonde, white, or even bluish gray. Bears are somewhat nearsighted, but they have a phenomenal sense of smell.

During the summer and fall, black bears need to eat enough food to gain up to 100 pounds of fat for the winter. They become voracious eaters to put on that extra weight.

Black bears are omnivores who eat vegetables and meat, just like humans. They like many of the same foods that people do. Bears have been known to break into houses in search of food. They will also tear into unattended food packs if campers don't keep them out of reach. Bears are wild animals, and therefore somewhat unpredictable, but they will often flee from humans, especially if those humans make a lot of noise.

Loon and Moon

Snake's Legs

Long ago, at the beginning of time, Snake was walking through the forest, smelling the air with her tongue. It might be hard to believe, but back then Snake had four legs and walked around like a fox or a lizard does now.

On this particular day, the sun blazed down on the forest and Snake was walking past the pond where Tadpole lived.

Tadpole looked admiringly at Snake's legs. He started thinking to himself, "Oooh, I would love to get some legs for myself. If I had legs, I could leap in the grass and chase bugs onto the land. If only I had legs like Snake."

You see, back in those days, tadpoles lived their whole lives in the water, like fish. Tadpole thought and thought all through the day and night about how he could get some legs. As the sun rose pink and gold in the east, Tadpole had his plan. When Snake walked by again, Tadpole was ready.

"Say Snake, how's it going? It looks mighty warm up there in the forest," said Tadpole.

It was a hot day and Snake was indeed feeling warm.

"Yessss," said Snake."It isss kind of warm up here."

"Hey!" Tadpole said, as if he had just thought of it. "Why don't you come for a swim in my pond? It's nice and cool."

Snake imagined how refreshing a dip in the pond would feel, but she had never learned to swim.

"Thanks for the invitation," Snake replied, "But I don't know how to swim."

"No problem," said Tadpole. "I'm an expert swimming instructor. I taught the fish how to swim. I taught the other tadpoles how to swim. I even taught the leeches how to swim."

That sounded promising, so Snake took a step closer to the pond.

"You have to take off your legs if you want to swim," warned Tadpole.

"That's a silly idea. Why must I do that?" asked Snake.

"Well, you see, it's a tradition," Tadpole explained. "Fish don't have legs, tadpoles don't have legs, and leeches definitely don't have legs. So if you want to swim, you will have to go legless."

Snake didn't want to take off her legs. You see she was very attached to them. So Snake decided not to learn to swim. But then Tadpole said something that made Snake reconsider.

"Listen, Snake. Not only is this water nice and cool, it's also magic. If you swim just once in my pond, you will never grow old."

Snake liked the sound of that. She was intrigued, but still doubtful.

"Really?" asked Snake.

"You've never seen an old tadpole, have you?" reasoned Tadpole.

That was enough evidence for Snake. She took off her four legs and hid them under a bush by the water. She wiggled on her belly into the pond.

Tadpole did just what he had promised. He taught Snake how to swim forward and backward, how to swim in a circle and dive deep in the pond. They swam from one end of that pond to the other. Snake loved the feel of the cool water on her scales. But after a long underwater dive, Snake surfaced on the far side of the pond. She looked around, but Tadpole had disappeared.

"Tadpole," called Snake. "Tadpole, where are you? Tadpole!"

Then Snake saw Tadpole wiggle out of the water on the far side of the pond, right next to her legs.

"Hey Tadpole, what are you doing? Get away from there! Those are MY legs!" yelled Snake, swimming across the pond.

Tadpole didn't pay any attention. He wiggled over to Snake's legs and stuck them on his body! But as Tadpole tried to run away, the back legs kept bumping against his tail. So Tadpole took off his tail and left it there, then he leaped off into the forest on Snake's legs.

When Tadpole had hopped deep into the forest, he began thinking to himself, "I'm not 'Tadpole' anymore. I have new legs and no tail. I'm a new animal, so I need a new name. Something snappy, something clever, something with one syllable."

You probably know what name he chose, right? He chose "Frog."

When Snake wiggled out of the pond, she found Tadpole's tail.

Loon and Moon

Trying to make the best of the situation, she added the tail to her already long, slim body. But Snake never forgave Tadpole and Frog for stealing her legs. From that day to this, whenever a snake catches a tadpole or frog, she eats it for dinner.

Now you might feel badly for Snake that she lost her legs, but maybe Tadpole wasn't lying about that magic water in the pond. To this day, there has never been a snake, or a tadpole, or even a leech with wrinkles.

Most snakes can swim and some species are positively at home in the water. Snakes are reptiles.

Frogs and toads are amphibians, which means "two lives." Tadpoles hatch from eggs in the water and look like fat fish at first. Then they start the process of metamorphosis, which means "changing shape." They slowly sprout legs, and their tails get shorter and finally disappear completely as they complete the transformation into a frog or toad. Some amphibians complete their metamorphosis in one summer; some complete the change in two summers. Worldwide, frog and toad numbers are declining. Increased pollution levels and habitat loss from filling wetlands for development are the major causes of the decline.

Loon and Moon

Slurp and the Mosquitoes

Long ago a terrible monster plagued the northwoods. He was big as a hill and was covered with hard green scales. He had black claws and sharp teeth and terrible long lips. His name was Slurp.

Now "Slurp" may not sound like a scary name for a monster, but he got that name from the terrible sucking sound that he made as he

SLLLUUURRRPED

up all of the water in a river, lake, puddle, or pond. When water animals heard that sound, it was the last sound they ever heard. When land animals heard that sound, they knew it was the beginning of the end for them as well. Without fresh, clean water to drink the animals had to leave, or die of thirst.

Barred Owl, with her sharp ears, had heard about Slurp, and when she saw Slurp slouching toward Big Lake, she knew she had to do something. She gathered up all of the animals for a meeting in the white pine woods.

"We've got to do something about this monster," said Barred Owl. "But whooo's going to do it? Whoo...Whoo...Who...Who?"

The animals looked at each other. Slurp was as tall as a white pine. He had sharp claws and teeth like the broken stones at the foot of the cliffs. No one wanted to get in Slurp's way. But if they were going to save their home, someone had to face the monster.

"Maybe he will only pass by and not drink up all our water," said Woodchuck hopefully.

"Not likely," grumbled Gray Bear. "If Slurp sees it, Slurp drinks it."

"Maybe we should fly to a land far from here," honked Goose.

Barred Owl just shook her head. "Slurp would still find us someday. And many of us can't fly."

The animals sighed and looked at the ground. Then huge Gray Bear let loose a growl. "I am the biggest and strongest of the animals. I will stop Slurp."

Gray Bear was bigger than Moose and stronger than anyone else in the forest. The animals were relieved that he had volunteered. If anyone could stop Slurp, surely Gray Bear could.

As the sun rose behind the eastern trees, turning the sky pink and gold, Gray Bear trudged down the path to the shore of Big Lake where Slurp was sleeping. The other animals hid in the bushes on the far side of the lake to watch. All day long the forest echoed with the growls and shouts of a great battle.

At twilight, when silence settled on the lake once more, the animals peered across the water. There in the moonlight, the animals could make out the shape of Slurp as he bent over the lake and began SLLLUUURRRPING up the water. Gray Bear was never seen again.

That night, the animals met again to decide what to do. "Gray Bear couldn't get rid of the monster, so maybe strength isn't the only thing we need," said Wolf. "Our wolf pack is both smart and strong. We will work together to get rid of Slurp."

The other animals knew the wolves were fearsome predators. They wished the pack good luck.

The next day, when the sun was high in the sky, the wolves crept up on the sleeping Slurp. They surrounded the monster, the same way they surround a moose. Then one of them ran up and bit Slurp on the leg.

"Oowwww!" roared Slurp and he kicked out with that leg, sending the wolf flying over the tallest pine trees.

Another wolf dashed in to grab Slurp's neck. But Slurp opened his mouth to roar, and the wolf was suddenly looking into a mouth like a huge cave with sharp stalactites and stalagmites. She ran back to the pack.

Loon and Moon

Seeing how powerful Slurp was, the wolves knew they were no match for the monster. They slunk back into the shadows of the trees and moved to a different part of the forest.

That night, the animals met again to discuss Slurp.

"If the strongest animal and the smartest animals can't get rid of Slurp, who can?" moaned Moose.

"Perhaps we should just leave the forest," said Woodchuck.

"Maybe we could trick Slurp into going somewhere else," mused Fox.

But then, amid all of the animal voices, a tiny whining voice spoke up. "Zzzeeeee. I'll stop the monster. Zzzeeeee. I'll stop the monster."

The animals looked around to see who was speaking and they saw that it was tiny Mosquito.

"Mosquito, you are so puny," said Chickadee. "You couldn't even hurt me. How could you possibly get rid of a huge monster like Slurp?"

"Size isn't everything. Zzzeeeee. I'll stop the monster. Zzzeeeee. I'll stop the monster," she insisted over and over again.

The animals were sure that Mosquito didn't have a chance against Slurp, but nobody else wanted to face the monster. They agreed to send her.

It was evening when Mosquito buzzed from shadow to shadow through the forest. When she came to the half-drained lake where Slurp was sleeping, she lowered her head and flew as fast as she could. She flew right up Slurp's nose! Immediately she began biting Slurp. He awoke with a start.

"Oowwww! Who's biting my nose?" Slurp yelled and blew a gust of wind out of his nostrils. Mosquito went flying halfway across the lake. But she was so small that in the darkness, Slurp couldn't see her. He searched all around, but couldn't find her, so he settled down to go back to sleep. Mosquito flew back and dove into Slurp's left ear. Slurp woke up again.

"Hey! Who's biting my ear?!" he roared. He scratched at his ear with his long claws. But he couldn't reach tiny Mosquito.

"Aaarg!" he howled. Then he splashed into what was left of the lake and dunked his head under the water. Mosquito swam out of

Slurp's ear and hid in the white petals of a water lily while her wings dried. When he couldn't find Mosquito again, Slurp figured she had drowned and he went back to sleep with snores that shook the trees.

Once her wings dried and she was able to fly again, Mosquito left her hiding place. She flew up into the air, dove into Slurp's right ear, and bit the big monster in a soft patch of skin.

"Ooww!" roared Slurp, slapping at his right ear. Slurp shook his head back and forth until Mosquito fell out. But Mosquito was so small that Slurp still couldn't find her.

Mosquito flew right back at Slurp, biting him on his eyelid, then his nose, and then his ears once again. But Slurp was getting smarter. He noticed that he could listen for Mosquito's whining wings. So he stood still and waited until Mosquito landed on his shoulder and then ... SLAP!

"Ho! Ho! Ho!" laughed Slurp. "Got that little bug."

But when Slurp raised his scaly paw, he didn't see a squished little bug. He saw two buzzing mosquitoes. The two mosquitoes buzzed and buzzed around Slurp's head and every time he slapped one of them, it turned into two more mosquitoes. Four, eight, sixteen, thirty-two mosquitoes buzzed and bit Slurp's ears, eyes, nose, neck, and paws. You see, back then Mosquito had magical powers and when you slapped one, it turned into two.

Finally, Slurp gave up. He turned and started running to the west, toward the setting moon. "Leave me alone! Leave me alone!" growled the monster in his gruffest voice.

But all that the mosquitoes would say, with a single voice, was "Zzzeee...leave our forest... zzzeee. Leave our forest...zzzeee..."

Slurp left. He ran across the dry prairies and all the way to the mountains with the mosquitoes right behind him. He ran into a cave and pulled a rock over the entrance to seal out his six-legged tormentors. And that was the last that anyone saw of Slurp.

As for Mosquito, when she and her family had finished chasing the monster, she returned to the northwoods and a hero's welcome. All of the birds and squirrels and deer and foxes cheered for the brave little Mosquito. But then Deer noticed that mosquito had been injured in the fight. She was bleeding and felt a little weak.

"Mosquito," said Deer. "Since you lost some of your blood

protecting us, you can take some of mine." The other animals offered their blood to Mosquito as well.

Even the ponds and swamps and puddles were grateful for what Mosquito had done. A small pond called out in a low, watery voice, "Mo-ski-toe, if you ever need a safe place to raise your children, bring them to me. I'll protect them."

And that is why it is to this day that female mosquitoes take blood from the other animals and why mosquitoes lay their eggs in the safety of ponds and swamps and puddles.

Now some people might think that it is annoying to have to deal with mosquitoes in the northwoods, but imagine what the world would be like if we had to contend with Slurp.

Many cultures tell stories about a gnat or mosquito or fly that overcomes a ferocious enemy. Most stories about mosquitoes talk about how terrible they are, but as a major food source for songbirds and fish, mosquitoes are important to the food chain.

Only a female mosquito bites. She uses the extra protein for additional energy as she produces 60-300 mosquito eggs. The itch from mosquito bites is an allergic reaction to mosquito saliva. That saliva also contains an anti-coagulant that keeps our blood from clotting while the mosquito is feeding.

Loon and Moon

The 3 Little Beavers

Once upon a time Bart Beaver, Becky Beaver, and Bucky Beaver lived with their parents in a lodge by the river. When they were two years old, which is almost grown up for a beaver, Mother Beaver told them, "It's time to find a home of your own." So the three little beavers set off swimming down the river.

As they were swimming, Becky Beaver saw a wolf sitting on the shore, licking his chops. It was B.B. (Big Bad) Wolf, a hungry fellow who was hoping for a tasty beaver dinner. Becky Beaver slapped her tail on the water to warn her brothers of danger, and they all dove under water and swam to the far side of the river. Bart and Becky felt relieved, but the encounter made Bucky think.

"We have to find homes soon," said Bucky Beaver. "If we don't have homes, we'll always have to watch out for wolves, day and night."

The little beavers swam downstream until they came to a grassy field.

"This looks like a lovely spot for me," said Bart Beaver, and he swam over to the riverbank to find a place for his home. Bart Beaver built himself a cozy house out of grass. At night he gathered up cattails and pond lilies to eat, and during the day he slept in his cozy grass home.

Becky and Bucky kept swimming downstream. Further down the river, Becky Beaver found a clump of alder trees. She chewed down the small trees and built herself a snug little house of sticks on the shore. In the evenings she nibbled bark from small branches, and during the day she slept in her snug little stick home.

Bucky Beaver liked the places his brother and sister had

chosen, but he wanted a house that would keep a wolf out. Further downstream he found a steep mud bank and a clump of aspen trees near the shore. Bucky started building a house of sticks, but that didn't seem strong enough. So he added mud and grass and stones to fill in the holes. When he finished, he had a strong, strong house. As he looked at the house, he realized he had made a mistake.

"I forgot to put a door in!" exclaimed Bucky.

But then Bucky thought, "If I put a door on land, anybody can get in. I'll put my door under water." So that is what he did. After a hard day of work, Bucky gathered some twigs, nibbled on the bark, and rested in his snug mud and stick home.

For a while, the three little beavers enjoyed their lives by the river, cutting down trees and eating bark, pond lilies, and cattails. But all that changed the day that B.B. Wolf followed his nose to Bart Beaver's grass house. When Wolf arrived, Bart Beaver was sound asleep.

"Hah! Grass can't stop a wolf like me. I'm strong as a mountain and tall as a tree!" Wolf laughed.

B.B. Wolf called out in his loudest voice, "Little Beaver, Little Beaver, let me come in!"

Bart Beaver woke up and felt his knees trembling. He squeaked out, "Not by the fur of my chinny-chin, chin."

"Then I'll stomp and I'll chomp and I'll pound your house in," said B.B. Wolf.

And that is exactly what he did. He stomped with his feet and chomped with his jaws and pounded on that house until it fell like rain in the springtime. As the grass house fell around him, Bart Beaver dashed out the back door and did a belly flop into the river. He swam as fast as he could, all the way to Becky Beaver's house.

A bit out of breath, Bart Beaver told his sister what had happened in the meadow. The two beavers ran inside Becky Beaver's stick house. They piled some extra sticks in the doorway.

Meanwhile, B.B. Wolf was searching through the rubble from the grass house, but he didn't find any beavers.

"Grrrr! He must have run out the back door and got away," growled Wolf. "I'll sniff and I'll snuff and I'll find that beaver,

soon enough."

It wasn't long before B.B. Wolf followed his nose to Becky Beaver's house. He crept up to the entrance.

"Hah! Sticks can't stop a wolf like me. I'm strong as a mountain and tall as a tree!" he laughed.

B. B. Wolf called out in his loudest voice, "Little Beaver, Little Beaver, let me come in!"

Bart Beaver dove into the corner to hide. Becky Beaver felt her knees trembling as she squeaked out, "Not by the fur of my chinny-chin, chin."

"Then I'll stomp and I'll chomp and I'll pound your house in," said B.B. Wolf.

And that is exactly what he did. He stomped with his feet and chomped with his jaws and pounded on that stick house until it fell like hail in the thunderstorm. As the house fell around them, Becky and Bart Beaver dashed out the back door and belly-flopped into the river. They swam all the way to Bucky Beaver's house.

When they arrived at their brother's lodge, Bucky Beaver was gathering cattails on the riverbank. Breathlessly, Bart and Becky told Bucky Beaver about the wolf.

"We'd better get inside," said Bucky Beaver. "I hid the door under water so a wolf couldn't find it."

The little beavers dove, swam to the entrance, and climbed into Bucky's sturdy home.

Meanwhile, back at the stick house, B.B. Wolf was searching through the rubble, but he didn't find any beavers. Then he sniffed the air.

"Arrg! They must have gone out the back door!" grumbled B.B. Wolf. "I'll sniff and I'll snuff and I'll find those beavers, soon enough."

B. B. Wolf followed his nose until he came to Bucky Beaver's mud, stone, and stick house.

"Hah! Mud can't stop a wolf like me, I'm strong as a mountain and tall as a tree!" he laughed.

B.B. Wolf called out in his loudest voice, "Little Beaver, Little Beaver, let me come in!"

Bart and Becky Beaver hid in the corner. But Bucky Beaver knew that his house was strong as a mountain. He called out in

his bravest voice, "Not by the fur of my chinny-chin, chin, you old windbag!"

That made Wolf angry. "Then I'll stomp and I'll chomp and I'll pound your house in," he yelled.

And that is exactly what he tried to do. He stomped with his feet and chomped with his jaws and pounded on the mud and stick house. But he couldn't knock it down. He looked for the door, but he couldn't find it. Wolf started feeling a little embarrassed. This had never happened to him before.

B.B. Wolf was feeling hungrier than ever. He couldn't believe a little beaver could build a lodge strong enough to keep him out, and he was longing for that delicious beaver dinner. So he took a deep breath and started again.

He stomped and he chomped, he dug and he tugged, he blew and he chewed and he pounded on the house, but nothing happened. Bucky Beaver's mud and stone and stick lodge really was as strong as a mountain.

Feeling confident, the three beavers swam out of their underwater door and into the middle of the river. B.B. Wolf was so hungry he jumped into the river after them. But, although wolves are good swimmers, they are not a match for beavers. The little beavers dove and came up far downstream. B.B. swam after them. The little beavers disappeared under water, then surfaced far upstream. B.B. gave up and swam to shore.

Too hungry to try any longer, B.B. Wolf growled, "I'll be back. You'll have to come onto land sometime." And he slunk into the forest in search of an easier meal.

From that day to this, beavers have had to be careful when they come onto land because B.B. Wolf is still lurking about, hoping for a tasty beaver dinner.

This is a northwoods retelling of the English tale, "The Three Little Pigs."

Wolves really do eat beavers, but wolves and other predators can usually only catch beavers on land. So beavers spend most of their time in or close to the water. They don't travel more than 100 yards from shore when felling trees. Beavers can stay under water for 15 minutes.

To avoid coming on land in the winter, beavers make a food cache (pronounced cash). They store lots of small branches under the water where they can reach them from their lodge without going out on the ice.

Beavers work together in matriarchal family groups, which means the mother is in charge. When you see a beaver slap its tail on the water, it is most likely the mother warning the rest of her family that danger is present. Young beavers go off to find their own territory when they are about two years old and their parents have had a new litter of kits.

Beavers build both lodges and dams of sticks and mud. The longest recorded beaver dam was 5,000 feet long - almost a mile!

Loon and Moon

Hawk and Grouse

At the very beginning of time, young Hawk and young Grouse were best friends. They went for walks together in the woods, they flew through the birch and aspen trees, and they played tag in the meadow. And even though Grouse was scatterbrained and she ate leaves and bugs, and Hawk was intense and she ate mice and voles, the two enjoyed each other's company. Even though they were very different, they were still the best of friends.

But as happens with all youngsters, Hawk and Grouse grew older. Soon it was time for them to make nests and lay their eggs. Grouse made her nest on the ground at the foot of an aspen tree at the edge of a meadow. Hawk made her nest high in the branches of a white pine tree in the forest. It was when Grouse was sitting on her eggs that she realized she had a problem.

You see, way back then when a chick hatched, it didn't have any feathers. Mother birds had to sew feather suits for their children to keep them warm. The problem was that while Grouse had been busy building her nest, she had lost her sewing needle. She looked all over for it. She looked under the grasses in the meadow, among the pine needles in the forest, and in the twigs near her nest. But she couldn't find it. Grouse was worried. "My eggs will hatch soon, and my children will need their feather coats," she thought. "Maybe I could ask Hawk for help. Surely she will lend me her sewing needle."

Grouse flew up to Hawk's nest. "Hey Hawk, how's it going?" said Grouse.

"Things are going well," said Hawk. "My new nest is done and I laid my eggs today. How are things going with you?"

"Well to tell you the truth, Hawk, I need a favor. I lost my

sewing needle and my chicks will be hatching any day now. Could I borrow yours? I only need it for a couple of days," pleaded Grouse.

Hawk wanted to help her friend, but she needed to make feather suits for her own chicks. After inspecting and listening to her eggs, Hawk decided she could wait a little while to begin sewing her suits.

"OK, Grouse, I will lend you my needle. But you have to promise to return it in two days. Remember, Grouse, two days."

"No problem, no problem," promised Grouse. "I'll have the needle back to you in two days, Hawk. Thanks a lot!"

Grouse took Hawk's silvery needle in her beak and flew off to her own nest. She sat down on her eggs and immediately started sewing feather suits for her ten children. It took Grouse a day and a half to make all of those suits.

Just as Grouse was finishing the last of her ten feather suits, she heard a

CRACK!

from her eggs. She jumped up to see one of her chicks poking its beak out of an egg. When the chick emerged, Mother Grouse pulled a feather suit over its head. Then she heard more cracking sounds and saw more chicks hatching.

As soon as the ten chicks had hatched and Grouse had dressed them in their feather suits, the chicks were hungry. They chirped and they cheeped until Mother Grouse took them out to the meadow to look for seeds and bugs. Then they were thirsty. They chirped and they cheeped until Mother Grouse took them to the stream to drink some water. Then they were cranky. Can you imagine that, children getting cranky? So Mother Grouse took them back to the nest for a nap. When they woke up, they did the same thing all over again: the field for bugs, the stream for water, and back to the nest for a nap. It can be difficult to care for one child, but imagine what it would be like with ten!

At the end of that busy day, Mother Grouse had the feeling in the back of her head that she had forgotten something. You know the feeling—like you haven't done something important. Just as

she was going to sleep, she remembered—Hawk's sewing needle! Mother Grouse got up and looked around the nest for the needle, but it was getting dark and she couldn't see a thing. Finally, she settled down and went to sleep.

The next morning, Mother Grouse gathered her chicks. "Now children, you need to help me look for a sewing needle that I borrowed from my friend Hawk to sew your feather suits," Mother Grouse explained. "It's small and silvery, so look closely at the ground."

The chicks scratched at the ground and pecked at the ground and looked all around the nest. But they didn't find the needle.

"We've spent a lot of time in the meadow, " said Mother Grouse. "Let's look there."

They searched all through the meadow, but looking for a sewing needle in a meadow is a lot like looking for a needle in a haystack. They didn't find it.

"Let's go look by the stream," said Mother Grouse feeling very nervous now.

They searched the stream banks and looked into the crystal clear water, but they didn't find the needle. That night, Mother Grouse told her chicks something she had never told them before: "Tonight children, we aren't sleeping in the nest. I want you to go into the aspen thickets and find a place to hide."

"But why, Mama?" whined the chicks.

And then Mother Grouse told her children something that parents have told children from the beginning of time. "Because I said so."

These chicks were obedient chicks and they did as their Mother told them. It was a good thing, too. Just as Mother Grouse was settling into her hiding place in the thicket, she saw Hawk fly over and land near Grouse's nest. Hawk looked around for her needle.

"Grouse! Grouse! Where's my needle?" shouted Hawk. "I said you could borrow it for two days. Two! Now it has been three, and my chicks are nearly ready to hatch! I need my needle!"

Now things might have turned out better if Grouse had just explained to Hawk what had happened. But Grouse wasn't that kind of friend. She was afraid, kind of a chicken. So she stayed hidden in the aspen trees.

"Grouse," called Hawk. "We have been friends, so I will give you one more day to bring back my needle."

And with that, Hawk opened her great wings and flew off.

The next day, Mother Grouse and her children searched for Hawk's sewing needle around the nest, in the meadow, and at the stream, but the more they looked, the less they found. When evening came, they went to hide under the aspen trees.

As the sun was setting, Hawk returned, circled three times over the meadow and landed near Grouse's nest. When Hawk didn't see her sewing needle, she called out to Grouse.

"Grouse, since you have stolen my sewing needle and I cannot make feather suits for my children, I will take the suits from yours. Whenever I see one of your chicks, I will grab it and take it to my nest. My children will wear the feathers from its skin and eat the meat from its bones. We are no longer friends!"

Again, Hawk opened her great wings and flew off.

And that is why to this day, whenever a hawk sees a grouse, the hawk swoops down and tries to catch the grouse for dinner. And whenever a grouse sees a hawk, she hides. And since that day, whenever you see a grouse, it is scratching and pecking at the ground. You might have thought that it is scratching the ground for bugs and pecking at seeds, but now you know the real reason. That grouse is searching for Hawk's sewing needle. Every grouse in the world is looking for that sewing needle in the hopes that if they return it, the hawks will stop hunting them.

Loon and Moon

This story is based on a tale from Kenya collected by a Peace Corps English teacher. The original story was called "Hawk and Chicken," but here it is adapted to the northwoods.

When many birds hatch from their eggs, they have downy feathers to keep them warm. Those that hatch without feathers quickly grow them after hatching. Over the next few weeks, baby birds begin to grow flight feathers. In one to two months, most birds fledge, which means they fly for the first time. Once a year most birds also molt, which means their old feathers fall out and new ones grow in to replace them. When this happens, some birds molt just a few feathers at a time and can keep flying. Others molt so many feathers that they stop flying for a short time.

Grouse are not strong flyers, usually flying only short distances to escape danger. They spend most of their time walking on the ground or perched in aspen trees feeding on buds and leaves.

Hawks are major predators of grouse. Other predators include great horned owls, barred owls, foxes, lynx, bobcats, and human hunters. Grouse depend on their camouflage coloration and ability to freeze, meaning "to hold very still so as to blend in with their surroundings." Predators may pass by without noticing a hidden grouse, unless they can smell it.

Loon and Moon

How Animals Got Their Colors

Long, long ago, before people walked this earth, every animal in the world was white like the fluffy clouds on a warm summer day. Every animal, from the smallest mouse to the largest moose, was white like the whitecaps on the lake when the strong wind blows. For a while, the animals didn't mind being white. But one day, Beaver started talking to himself.

"You know, I don't like being a white beaver. No, I want to be something different, like... like purple. Yeah, that's what I want to be—a purple beaver."

Once beaver started talking, other animals heard him and began thinking about new colors that they could be. Deer started thinking to herself, "White is just too plain. I want something more dramatic, like red. Red would be a great color for deer."

And then there were the butterflies.

"It's so hard to find a husband these days," said Monarch. "Whenever I fly up to a male butterfly, he's the wrong species."

Monarch's friends agreed.

"If only there were a way to tell the right ones from the wrong ones," sighed Swallowtail.

Soon every animal in the forest wanted a new color, but nobody knew how to get one. Sometimes when people don't know how to solve a problem, they hold a meeting, and that's exactly what the animals did. They met in a huge clearing and Owl, the wisest animal in the forest, led the meeting.

"Whooo has an idea? Whooo has a suggestion?" asked Owl.

Chipmunk raised her little paw.

"I've got an idea, I've got a really, really good idea, how about we get some bright colors like red and yellow and green and blue and purple and color ourselves all over with stripes and circles and polka dots and everything what do you think about that?" chattered Chipmunk, all in one breath.

Many of the animals weren't quite sure what Chipmunk had said because she talked so fast, but they heard the word "color" and all the color names, and they liked that.

"Colors, yes! We want colors! We like colors! Yes! Yes!" cheered the animals.

"Whooo else has an idea?" called Owl, hoping someone else would speak more slowly.

Eagle raised her wing. "I have seen colors we could use, way up in the sky. After it rains, huge bands of color stretch from one end of the sky to the other. Every color in the world is there—red, orange, yellow, green, blue, indigo, and violet. We birds could fly up there and get the colors," suggested Eagle.

The animals didn't have a name for those bands of color, but you do. You call them rainbows. The birds liked that plan, but the walking animals weren't quite so certain.

"Hey wait a minute," said Bear. "What's to keep you birds from flying off with the colors and not bringing any back to the rest of us animals?"

Then Beaver spoke up.

"Hey guys, I've got an idea. I'm a beaver and I chop down trees. I think that if I find an aspen tree tall enough, and line it up just right, I could make it fall on those bands of color and knock them to the ground."

The animals liked that plan. They liked the plan because it was simple. They liked it because it would bring colors to the ground where everyone could reach them. But they especially liked it because Beaver would do most of the work. The animals agreed that Beaver would get the colors for them.

You know how it is when you are waiting for something like a birthday or a vacation—it always seems to take forever to come. That's the way it was while the animals waited for a rainbow. Days went by without rain. Weeks went by without rain. There was no

Loon and Moon

rain for so long that some animals started to think it might never rain again. But finally one morning, thick gray clouds covered the eastern sky. Squirrel saw them and called to the other animals.

"Rain! Rain! It's going to rain! Everybody get ready!"

Chipmunk was so excited she began running laps inside her burrow. Deer lay down beneath a maple tree and imagined how beautiful she would look with rich red fur. The songbirds began chirping and flapping their white wings. Snake just lay still, flicking her tongue in and out. Beaver began sharpening his long front teeth.

At first just a few drops fell, then sprinkles pattered on the leaves and began to drip down the grass stems. At last the rain came pouring down in sheets. Trails turned into streams and low spots turned into puddles. Finally the clouds broke apart and, although it was still raining, the sun began to shine. Then, just as Eagle had said, huge bands of color stretched from one end of the sky to the other.

Beaver swam out of his lodge and then waddled onto shore and over to the aspen tree he had saved for this moment. It was a big one that reached all the way to the sky. Beaver lined it up with the rainbow and started chewing. The other animals gathered behind Beaver. Even though they were eager to get colors, they knew better than to stand in front of a beaver who was chopping down a tree. When the tree was chewed halfway through, it began to lean and crack until

FUWUUMMPPP!

it crashed right into the rainbow. That rainbow broke into a million pieces. As the colors rained down from the sky, the animals flew or hopped or ran toward them, splashing through the puddles.

The birds got to the colors first. Goldfinch found yellow and painted himself from beak to tail. Jay grabbed some blue to color his feathers. Cardinal splashed red all over himself. These were only the male birds because it was spring and the females were busy sitting on their nests. Female birds didn't have time for foolish things like colors.

The flying insects came next. Dragonflies chose turquoise for

How Animals Got Their Colors

their bodies. The bees and wasps picked gold and black. Lady beetles took some crimson and the tiger beetles grabbed the green. Butterflies came in family groups. All of the Monarchs decided to be orange with black lines. The Tiger Swallowtails decided on yellow with black lines. When the cabbage butterflies saw everyone else getting colors, they decided to stay white. By the time the birds and flying insects had taken their colors, most of the brightest colors were either used up or had mixed together in puddles on the ground and turned brown or gray.

Beaver looked all over for some purple, but the purple martins and wood ducks had taken the last of it. Then he saw a big piece of orange sticking out of the grass. He ran over and grabbed it with his teeth. But it was stuck. Beaver tugged and tugged until finally a piece broke off, all over his teeth. That colored his teeth orange, but didn't do anything for his fur. Beaver decided that brown would be a good enough color for him, so he rolled in some dark brown that he found in a puddle.

Deer couldn't find any red for her fur, so she decided, "If I can't have a dramatic color, then I will at least paint myself in a dramatic way."

She found some tan in a puddle and painted her head, back, and legs, but left her belly and tail white. She admired herself in the still waters of a pond.

"Perfect," she thought.

By this time, the brightly colored male birds had gone back to their nests so the females could come looking for colors. But when they arrived even most of the brown colors were used up. So the female birds settled for having brown speckles on their feathers. When the disappointed females returned to their nests, their mates gave them hugs and some of the bright colors on the males rubbed off on the females as well.

As the sun was setting, the very slowest of the creatures, like slug and snail, came to the place where the colors had fallen. These creatures could only find the grays and the blacks, so those are the colors they are today.

Now some people say that all the colors didn't go to the animals on that day. They say that some of the colors leaked into cracks in

Loon and Moon

the earth. Each spring, those colors come back as the violet, pink, yellow, and blue wildflowers that grow here each spring.

Other people say that not every animal heard about the plan. Those animals that live far to the north, like Polar Bear and Arctic Wolf and Arctic Fox, are still white to this day because they didn't know about the day when Beaver got colors from the sky.

Many cultures have stories about how animals got their colors and markings.

Animals have their colors for many reasons. Some male birds have bright colors so they can attract a mate and show off to other male birds. Many female birds have dull colored feathers so they will blend in with their surroundings when sitting on their nests. Other birds like turkeys and grouse have dull colors so they can hide from predators. The bright colors of some animals, like ladybugs and monarch butterflies, seem to warn predators that these animals will taste bad.

Some animals change their color. In the summer, snowshoe hares are brown. In autumn, as the days get shorter, their fur changes to white, helping them to blend in with the snowy winter woods and hide from their enemies. In spring, as the snow melts, the brown fur grows back in slowly.

Loon and Moon

The 3 Buck Brothers

Once upon a time at the edge of a deep, deep woods, there lived three buck brothers. The youngest of these brothers was a spike buck, with only two little antlers on his head. The middle brother was a four-point buck, and the oldest of the brothers was an eight-point buck. The three buck brothers fed on the grass and green twigs in their meadow in the hills above the great river. But one summer, the sun beat down with a strength that made the grass and shrubs wilt and turn brown. The buck brothers had a harder and harder time finding enough to eat.

Spike, hungry and longing for some fresh green leaves, thought, "There must be better leaves and grass somewhere! I'm going to look for a better meadow."

Spike looked from the highest hilltop and saw a luscious green meadow on the banks of a stream on the far side of the great river. He thought to himself, "There's probably plenty of tasty, sweet, green grass down there. I just have to find a way across the river."

Now deer can swim well, but this river flowed faster than a hunting hawk, and the water foamed and splashed over rapids and waterfalls. Any deer that tried to cross the river could be swept downstream to the great waterfall and never be seen again. So Spike searched up and down the river for a safe place to cross. He soon found a huge pine log that bridged the water. Spike climbed up on the log and walked

TRIP TRAP
TRIP TRAP
TRIP TRAP

across the river. But when he was half way across, a huge wildcat leaped onto the log .

"Yum, yum, yeep!" growled Mountain Lion. "I LOVE to eat deer meat!"

Spike was startled, but his mind was as quick as his feet.

"Oh, Mr. Lion," he said. "I am just a tiny spike buck, hardly worth the trouble to chase. If deer meat is what you love, then you should wait a bit. My older brother Bill is on his way here. He is much bigger than I am and he would make a satisfying meal."

Mountain Lion hesitated. Spike was kind of small, and a nice big deer would make a nice big meal.

Lion thought, "This deer is so scrawny, I'd better let him fatten up in the green meadow. Besides, I can always catch him when he comes this way again."

"You're sure he will be coming this way?" growled Mountain Lion.

"Oh yes, I'm sure he will be looking for tasty green grass, just like I am," said Spike.

"Well then," said Lion, licking his chops. "You can go… this time."

A little while later the four-point buck, Billy, noticed that Spike was gone and decided to look for him.

"That little buck is always getting into trouble," thought Billy as he walked through the forest. Billy came to the log across the great river. He noticed the fresh green grass on the other side, and he saw Spike's tracks in the sand by the river.

Billy started across the log with a "trip-trap, trip-trap." But when he was half way across, Mountain Lion leaped onto the log growling, "Yum, yum, yeep! I LOVE to eat deer meat!"

Billy thought fast.

"Well, Mr. Lion, you could eat me. But I'm sure I would be nothing but a snack for such a great hunter as you. Why don't you wait for my older brother? He is much bigger than I am, and he would make a splendid feast," said Billy.

"I've heard this before," thought Mountain Lion. But then he thought some more. "If that older brother is big and tasty, I can always come back and catch this one for dessert."

"You're sure your brother is coming this way?" asked Mountain Lion.

"Oh, yes, he'll be along any minute looking for my younger brother and me," said Billy.

"Okay, then you can go... this time," said Lion.

Billy walked across the log and over to the shady meadow where Spike was eating grass. It wasn't long before the eight-point buck, William, noticed that his two younger brothers weren't around. He began searching the forest until he came to the great river and the huge log. He noticed the green grass on the other side, and two sets of deer tracks in the sand.

William started across the river with a "trip-trap, trip-trap." But when he was half way across, Mountain Lion leaped onto the log growling, "Yum, yum, yum, yeep! I LOVE to eat deer meat!"

William had dealt with mountain lions before, and he was ready.

"Well, Mr. Lion, I guess you have me. But since you are going to eat me anyway, let's make this quick. How about you stand there and open your mouth wide, and I will leap right into it," said William.

Lion figured this would save a lot of energy. After all, it was hard work to chase animals. And he could almost taste the delicious meal he was about to swallow.

Lion opened his mouth so wide that William could see Lion's back teeth. He open his mouth so wide that his eyes squinched shut. With his eyes shut, Lion didn't see William lowering his antlers. William charged at Mountain Lion. Bam! He slammed

into the lion, smashing Lion's teeth and knocking him into the fast-flowing river. The foaming water washed Lion downstream, never to be seen again.

Then William finished crossing the log "trip-trap, trip-trap," and walked over to the shady meadow where his brothers were eating. The three buck brothers ate their fill and they lived happily, and cleverly, ever after.

This is a northwoods version of the traditional Norwegian tale, The Billy Goats Gruff.

Mountain lions, also called cougars or panthers or pumas, hunt and eat deer, often pouncing from trees or stalking them before giving chase. While you might think that a powerful predator like a mountain lion would be able to catch any deer that it wanted to, this isn't true. Large predators usually have abysmal hunting success rates. Researchers estimate that in North America, predators only catch 10 percent of the prey they chase. Since it takes a lot of energy to chase, catch, and subdue large prey animals like deer, predators often choose the easiest prey they can find: the very young, the very old, and the sick or injured.

It's Your Turn to Tell Stories

Here are some ideas to get you started telling stories of your own:

• To develop your story-telling skills, start with something short, easy, and familiar. Perhaps you could tell about how your pet got its name, or how you learned to swim or ride a bike, or your favorite holiday tradition.

• Find some words for your story that sound like what is happening - like the words "slurp" and "trip trap" in this book.

• Add a little dialog, which means words that someone was thinking or saying.

• When you tell the story, vary your voice to show excitement or slowness or shyness or whatever your characters are feeling.

• Tell your story out loud several times, until you can say it almost the same way each time. You don't need a person to listen to you - tell it to a tree, or a pet, or the sky.

• When you are ready for an audience, tell your story to a younger child or to a grandparent or older friend. They are usually good listeners.

• Make up stories for things you wonder about, like why the ants all move in a line, or how the plants grow through the cracks in a sidewalk, or where your cat goes when she's not in your backyard. Keep the stories short to start with, so you can remember them.

• Ask other people to tell you stories. You might have to suggest a topic, like the biggest storm they remember, or their favorite teacher, or a trip they took.

• One more hint: turn off the television, the computer, the ipod, and the cell phone. Listen and talk to real people in real time. You might be amazed as well as amused.

Also Available From Raven Productions:

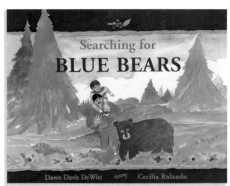

Searching for Blue Bears
A young boy learns about black bears while looking for the blue bears everyone is talking about. He finally finds his blue bears when Grandma takes him berry picking.

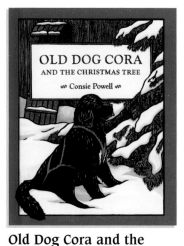

Old Dog Cora and the Christmas Tree
An older Newfoundland Retriever envies her pups in harness, but finds her own way to help with holiday preparations.

But Grandma Didn't Mind and **But That's OK with Grandpa**
Spending time with Grandma and Grandpa includes a few mishaps in these charming books illustrated with photos from the 1950's. These books will prompt grandparents to share their memories with the family.

For more details and other titles, visit our website:

www.ravenwords.com